Praise for The Imagination Station® books

Our children have been riveted and on the edge of their seats through each and every chapter of The Imagination Station books. The series is well-written, engaging, family friendly, and has great spiritual truths woven into the stories. Highly recommended!

—Crystal P., *Money Saving Mom*®

Secret of the Prince's Tomb is my favorite book! It has great action and adventure. It is better than any book I have ever read . . . and I read a lot!

—Luke, age 9, Allendale, New Jersey

[The Imagination Station books] focus on God much more than the Magic Tree House books do.

—Emilee, age 7, Waynesboro, Pennsylvania

These books will help my kids enjoy history.

—Beth S., third-grade public school teacher
Colorado Springs, Colorado

More praise for *The Imagination Station®* books

These books are a great combination of history and adventure in a clean manner perfect for young children.

—Margie B., *My Springfield Mommy* blog

My nine-year-old son has already read [the first two books], one of them twice. He is very eager to read more in the series too. I am planning on reading them out loud to my younger son.

—Abbi C., mother of four, Minnesota

FOCUS ON THE FAMILY® PRESENTS

THE IMAGINATION STATION®

Secret of the Prince's Tomb

BOOK 7

**MARIANNE HERING • MARSHAL YOUNGER
CREATIVE DIRECTION BY PAUL McCUSKER
ILLUSTRATED BY DAVID HOHN**

TYNDALE

FOCUS ON THE FAMILY • ADVENTURES IN ODYSSEY
TYNDALE HOUSE PUBLISHERS, INC. • CAROL STREAM, ILLINOIS

ISBN: 978-1-58997-673-3

A Focus on the Family book published by Tyndale House Publishers, Inc.,
Carol Stream, Illinois 60188

Focus on the Family and Adventures in Odyssey, and the accompanying
logos and designs, are federally registered trademarks, and The Imagination
Station is a federally registered trademark of Focus on the Family, Colorado
Springs, CO 80995.

TYNDALE and Tyndale's quill logo are registered trademarks of Tyndale
House Publishers, Inc.

With the exception of known historical figures, all characters are the product
of the authors' imaginations.

Cover design by Michael Heath | Magnus Creative

Cataloging-in-Publication Data for this book is available by contacting the
Library of Congress at http://www.loc.gov/help/contact-general.html.

Printed in the United States of America
1 2 3 4 5 6 7 8 9 / 16 15 14 13 12

For manufacturing information regarding this product, please
call 1-800-323-9400.

To Peggy Wilber,

who taught my son to read and how to

have fun while learning. —MKH

Contents

The Imagination Station

It was the end of summer. Patrick pushed open the door to Whit's End. The bell above the ice-cream-shop door jingled.

Patrick's cousin Beth followed him.

Patrick went to the counter and sat down. His face was red. He was breathing hard.

A friendly looking man with white hair and a white moustache stood behind the counter. He was cleaning a glass. His name was John Avery Whittaker. Some adults called him Whit. He looked up at the two cousins and smiled.

"Hello, Patrick," Whit said. "Hi, Beth."

Beth climbed onto a stool next to Patrick.

"Hi, Mr. Whittaker," Beth said.

Whit eyed Patrick. "Is everything all right, Patrick?"

Patrick frowned. "No," he said.

Whit put down the glass. "What's wrong?"

Patrick clenched his hands together. He fumed.

"School starts next week. Patrick is mad about it," Beth explained.

Whit chuckled. "I remember how hard it was to see vacations end," he said.

"I don't like school," Patrick said.

Whit gazed at Patrick. "What don't you like about it?" Whit asked.

"It's hard work. Everyone bosses me around. The kids tease me," Patrick said.

Whit nodded. "I understand," he said warmly. "But you know the hard work is to help you learn. And getting 'bossed around' is part of being taught. It's about discipline and responsibility."

"I don't like it," Patrick said. "Especially after summer break. We got to do whatever we wanted."

"I know what you mean," Whit said. He turned to Beth. "Is that how you feel?" Whit asked.

"Mostly. But I'm looking forward to seeing my friends again," Beth said.

"That's because you have a lot of friends," Patrick said. "I have only a few. The rest of the time I get teased."

Whit asked Patrick, "What do they tease you about?"

Patrick shrugged. "Almost everything," he said. "I'm not as good at sports as some of them. And I'm not as smart as some of the others. It's the smart ones who bother me the most."

Whit asked, "About what?"

Patrick thought for a moment. "Some of

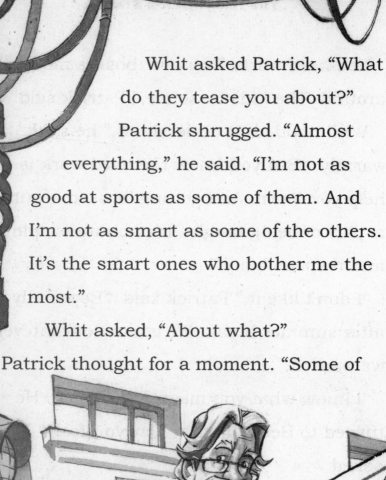

them say I'm stupid. It's all because I believe in God," he said.

Whit's eyebrows wrinkled together with concern. "They tease you about your faith?" he asked.

"A few kids in the science club are proud of themselves. They brag that they don't believe in God," Patrick said. "They know that I do, so they tease me about it."

"You, too?" Whit asked Beth.

"Sometimes," she replied.

Whit rubbed his chin. "That's too bad," he said.

"It's like they won't be happy until I believe the way they do," Patrick said.

Whit leaned on the counter. "People who don't believe in God are often bothered by those who do. Or they believe in other gods. It's happened throughout history," he said. "Some people are made slaves for their beliefs."

"That's how I feel about school," Patrick said. "I feel like I'm a slave. Teachers make us work hard."

Whit put his hand over his mouth. Beth thought he was going to laugh.

"I don't think you know much about

slavery. Or you wouldn't say things like that," Whit said.

"I was a slave in one of the Imagination Station trips," Beth said. "It was hard."

Patrick shrugged. "I'm just telling you how I feel," he said.

"And where do you think God is while you're feeling this way?" Whit asked. A smile hung around his lips. "Has He disappeared? Has He abandoned you to the terrible suffering you have at school?"

Patrick looked at Whit. "Now *you're* teasing me," he said.

"I'm just wondering," Whit said.

Patrick slowly shook his head.

Whit stroked his moustache. He often did that when he had an idea. "How would you two like a trip in the Imagination Station?"

Whit asked.

"I'd love to go!" Beth said. She leaped from the stool.

"I guess," Patrick said as he slid from his stool. "Are you going to make me a slave to teach me how bad it is?"

Whit smiled. "No. I have another idea," he said.

He led the cousins to the basement workshop.

They entered a large room filled with inventions and tools. The Imagination Station sat in the corner.

The Imagination Station was bubble-shaped like the front part of a helicopter. It had sliding doors on two sides. Inside were two seats and a control panel. It was kind of like a time machine.

Whit opened a panel on the side and began typing on a small computer there.

"So where are we going this time?" Beth asked.

"You'll find out when you get there," Whit said. "Get in."

Patrick and Beth climbed into the cockpit. "What about our costumes?" they asked.

"I changed the program," Whit said. "The clothes you're wearing will change. They will look right for the time. And you'll have a few other things you'll need."

"Cool!" Beth said.

Patrick looked as if he were already coming out of his bad mood.

"Ready?" Whit said.

"We're ready," Beth said. She held up a thumb to signal okay.

"Then press the red button," Whit said.

Beth pressed it.

The machine started to shake. Then it rumbled. It seemed to move forward.

Then the rumble grew louder.

The machine whirred.

Suddenly, everything went black.

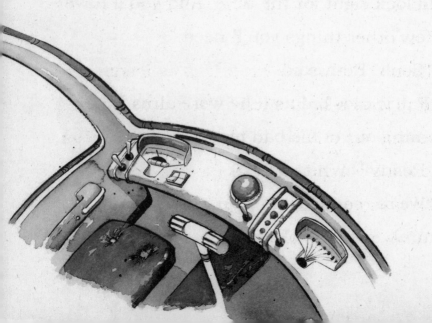

The Marketplace

The Imagination Station stopped like a car at the end of a rollercoaster ride. Beth's head bobbed forward. She looked around at the darkness.

Then there was light. It was as if someone had flipped a light switch. Beth was blinded. She held up a hand to block the brightness. Then she glanced over at Patrick.

He was covering his eyes too.

"What is it?" she asked.

"The sun," he said.

Beth was aware of the heat now. Then the sounds of voices.

The cousins were sitting on the ground. Someone bumped her. A crowd of people bustled around them.

"Where are we?" Patrick asked.

Beth stood up and brushed herself off. She looked down. She was wearing a thin, long white dress. It felt like a bedsheet on her skin.

Patrick stood and then peered down as well. He was dressed in a tunic.

Beth giggled. Patrick's tunic looked like a skirt. She looked at the crowd. All of the men wore tunics like Patrick's.

The cousins both wore large, beautiful gold collars and gold belts.

Patrick pulled at his collar. "It's so hot," he said.

Beth agreed. She felt as if she were in an oven.

The cousins seemed to be in everyone's way. They were bumped and jostled. Tents and tables were set up all around them. It was a marketplace.

Beth sniffed the air. Something smelled like dead fish and overripe fruit.

No one else seemed to notice the foul smell.

Then Beth saw a man with a basket of fish, grapes, and bread. He put it onto the right arm of a balance scale.

Another man sat behind the scale. He stood up. He carefully placed metal balls on the left arm of the scale. He was weighing the man's food to see how much it cost.

"Four *deben*," the man said.

Patrick moved toward a table filled with knives and arrows. He picked up a knife and showed it to Beth.

The knife had a gold handle. The handle had a figure carved in it. It showed a man's body with the face of a dog.

"I've seen these in books," Patrick said. "I know where we are, Beth. We're in Egypt! That's an image of one of their gods."

Beth nodded. Her gaze went to a table with clay jars. Each of them had something different on top. One had a dog's head, one a bird, one an alligator, and one a man's head.

She also saw beautiful vases. All of them had strange half-man, half-animal figures on the sides.

Beth reached into a pocket in her tunic. She hoped the Imagination Station had given her some money to spend. Instead, she felt something else.

"Hey, Patrick," Beth said. She held up a small book. "I had this in my tunic."

Patrick looked at the book.

"It's about hieroglyphics," Beth said. "It's full of Egyptian picture-words."

Patrick reached into his tunic. He found a small book too. "It's a Bible," he said.

A thin braided string stuck out of the top. "There's a bookmark," Beth said.

Patrick flipped through the pages. "Maybe this will explain what's going on," he said.

Suddenly, a girl with beautiful dark hair ran up to them. She wore a colorful dress.

"Pretend to be my friends," the girl said.

Beth and Patrick looked at each other. They had no idea who this girl was.

"Talk to me like I'm your friend," she said.

Patrick shrugged. He said, "Oh, look at this musical instrument. It looks like a five-stringed harp."

"Yes," the girl said. "The strings are made from goose entrails."

"Gross," Beth said. "Goose guts."

"Cool!" Patrick said.

The girl glanced behind her nervously. "Oh no! They're coming!"

"Who?" Patrick asked.

"Egyptian guards! They're trying to kidnap me!" she said. "I must hide!"

Across the marketplace, Beth saw stern-looking men. They were dressed in white tunics. Their arms were bare, and they had large collars around their necks. They had swords.

Patrick pointed to a group of camels tied together by rope. The animals had baskets, pots, or barrels strapped to their humps.

"Quick! We can hide behind the camels," Patrick said.

The three children hustled toward the camels. The guards arrived. They searched around the merchants' tables.

"You're safe," Beth said to the girl.

Then an Egyptian woman took the lead camel's rope. She began to walk the beasts away from the market.

"What do we do?" the girl asked.

"Walk with them," Patrick said.

The children stayed behind the camel train. The woman led the camels down a side street.

Then a man's deep voice called out, "There she is!" The man was pointing at them.

"Run!" the girl said.

The three kids took off down the narrow street. They ducked around the corner of a building. They stopped behind a large statue.

Suddenly, a hand thrust out in front of them. It grabbed the girl by her shoulder. She screamed.

"Tabitha," the man said gently. He took her in his arms.

"Father," the girl said. She rested her head against his chest.

"We must hurry home," the man said. "There's big trouble."

Tabitha's House

Patrick's mouth fell open when he saw Tabitha's house. In the front, nine columns held up a high roof.

Those columns are as thick as hundred-year-old trees, Patrick thought.

Inside, the ceilings were as high as the gym at their school. The brick floor was painted with bright blues and greens. Large plants in vases lined the halls.

Farther in, more columns surrounded

a courtyard. There was a tub of water made out of stone. It looked like a shallow swimming pool.

Patrick suddenly noticed how hot he was. His skin felt itchy and sweaty. He wanted to jump into that water.

Tabitha's father pointed to a side room. "Gather your most important things," he told Tabitha.

"Why, Father?" Tabitha asked.

Her father didn't answer. He raced into another room. Beth and Patrick followed Tabitha into the side room.

Tabitha went to a trunk. She pulled out some clothes. Then she went to a bed with a wooden frame and ropes strapped across it. The "pillow" was a wood block.

That doesn't look comfortable, Patrick
thought.

Tabitha reached under the bed. She
pulled out a small doll and put it with
her clothes.

Tabitha's father suddenly cried out.

The children rushed from the room.

Two large, brown-skinned men were in
the courtyard. They held Tabitha's father
by the arms.

"This is no longer your home," one of
the men said. His neck was thick. A gold
collar circled it.

"Our family has lived in this house for
generations," Tabitha's father said.

"There are new rules for the Habiru.
Even the rich ones," the man said. "Your
days of living like royalty are over."

"This is robbery!" Tabitha's father shouted. He struggled. The man grabbed him and pushed him toward the door.

"Father!" Tabitha cried. She ran to her father.

The other large man grabbed Tabitha and picked her up. She squirmed in his arms.

"Put me down!" Tabitha cried.

The men took them out of the courtyard and into a hallway. They headed for the front door.

"Should we do something?" Patrick asked Beth.

"What can we do?" Beth said. "Those guys are huge!"

The cousins followed them outside.

"Stop!" came a small voice.

The large men obeyed.

Patrick saw a child dressed in a white skirt. He wore a beautiful golden collar too. The collar was shaped like a mighty bird.

The boy was almost bald. A single braid grew from the top center of his head. The braid was long enough to reach his shoulder.

The boy spoke. "What are you doing?" he asked the large men.

"We have orders to drive these Habiru out," one of the men said. "They are no longer welcome to live here. They will join the rest of their people."

The boy pointed at Tabitha. "She is my friend," he said. "And her father is an important official in the court. You will leave them alone."

The two large men glanced at each other. They put Tabitha on the ground and let go of her father. Saluting the boy, they turned and walked off without a word.

Patrick looked at the boy. *Why are these huge guys listening to that little kid?* he wondered.

The boy took Tabitha's hand. "Are you all right?" he asked her.

"Yes," Tabitha said, smiling at him. "Thank you."

The boy let go of Tabitha's hand. He looked at Beth and Patrick. "Who are you?" he asked.

"I'm Patrick. And this is my cousin Beth," Patrick said.

"I am Lateef," the boy said.

"Guards tried to grab me at the marketplace," Tabitha said. "They wanted to put me to work digging with the other Habiru. But Patrick and Beth helped me escape."

The boy nodded at the cousins. "I'm grateful," he said. "It's unusual for strangers to help the Habiru."

"Is there something wrong with the Habiru?" Beth asked.

"There wasn't," Lateef said. "But something has changed."

Tabitha frowned. "You're safer away from us," she said to Beth and Patrick.

Tabitha's father nodded. "We must be careful," he said. "At least until I know why my people are being treated this way.

Many have already been taken out of their homes."

"Where should we go?" Beth asked.

"Come with me," Lateef said. He turned and walked away.

The cousins said good-bye to Tabitha and left the house. They had to run to catch up with Lateef.

He looked angry. "I will speak with my father about sparing Tabitha's family," the boy said.

"Who is your father?" Patrick asked as they walked.

Lateef's mouth fell open. "You don't know?" he said. "My father is the pharaoh!"

The Nile

"The pharaoh?" Beth asked. "You mean, kind of like the king?"

"Yes," Lateef answered. "I'll ask him why the entire country has turned against the Habiru."

Lateef walked very quickly now.

Beth and Patrick jogged to keep up with Lateef.

They passed a wide river. Many people sat and watched the water. Beth wondered why they looked so concerned. A few were crying.

"What are they looking at?" Beth asked.

"The Nile River is too low," Lateef said.

"How much too low?" Patrick asked.

Lateef motioned toward the water. "Do you see the lines on the riverbank?" Lateef asked.

The cousins nodded. Fat black lines were painted on the sides of the rocks.

Lateef said, "If the water doesn't rise, the Nile won't flood enough. What you're standing on is called the Black Land."

"Looks green to me," Patrick said.

Lateef ignored him. "The Nile floods every year. That makes the Black Land more fertile. If the river doesn't flood, the land dries out. Then the ground you're standing on becomes like the Red Land."

"Is the Red Land the desert?" Beth asked.

Lateef nodded. "The crops won't grow," he said. "We'll have a terrible famine."

"My father says not to worry about things you can't control," Patrick said.

"But we can control this," Lateef said.

"You can *make* it rain?" Beth asked.

Lateef said, "Yes."

Beth glanced at Patrick. It looked as if he was holding back a laugh.

"How can you do that?" Beth asked.

"I have to show you," Lateef said.

Lateef took them to a huge building. Its columns made the columns in Tabitha's house look like toothpicks. Hieroglyphics decorated every column and every wall.

"This is the temple," Lateef said. "We're allowed on the patio. Only the priests may go all the way inside."

People scurried about. Their faces were turned down with sadness. They carried bowls of sweet-smelling incense. Many brought in small pieces of cloth with hieroglyphics on them.

"What are they doing?" Patrick asked.

"They are offering sacrifices to the gods," Lateef answered. "They bring their gifts to the temple. Prayers are written on the cloths. Then the priest offers the gifts and prayers to the gods inside."

"Which gods?" Beth asked.

"Ra, the god of the sun." Lateef pointed to a picture of a man on the wall. The man had the head of a bird. The sun was on top of his head.

"Seth, the god of storms," Lateef said. He

pointed to a picture of a man. The man had a strange-looking horse head.

"And Anuket, the goddess of the Nile." He pointed to a picture of a woman. She wore a tall gold headdress.

"Exactly how many gods do you have?" Beth asked.

"We have hundreds of gods," Lateef said.

Beth had learned about Egypt's gods in school. But she still thought this was very strange. She believed in only one God. He was the one who created the universe and everything in it.

Lateef continued. "If the

people bring enough sacrifices, the gods will be happy. Then, if the gods choose, they will raise the waters. The gods might save us. They might send rain."

"Why aren't your gods happy?" Patrick asked.

"Many things can make them angry," Lateef said. "Only one thing pleases them: sacrifice."

Patrick and Beth exchanged worried looks.

Lateef took them back to the marketplace. He bought some fish and gave one to each of them. Beth held the slimy creature with two fingers.

"We must go back to the temple," Lateef said. "You will offer your sacrifice there."

"I won't offer a sacrifice," Patrick said. He handed the fish back to Lateef.

"Why not?" Lateef asked.

Beth glanced at Patrick. *Patrick had better be careful here. This is the pharaoh's son. He could get us in a lot of trouble!*

Patrick said, "We have our own God. We can't sacrifice to yours."

Lateef stepped forward. He glared at Patrick. "You refuse to bow to our gods? Say so, and these will be the last words you ever speak."

The Pharaoh

Patrick looked into Lateef's face. The pharaoh's son meant business.

What should I say? Patrick wondered. *If I say the wrong thing, he'll have me killed.*

But there was no way Patrick would sacrifice to the Egyptian gods. Then he had an idea.

"Is it a crime to worship one God?" Patrick asked quickly. "Do you mean no one here worships just one God?" He could feel Lateef's hot breath on his face.

"The Habiru do," Lateef said. "And my people don't trust them because of that."

"But your friend Tabitha worships one God?" Beth asked.

"Yes," Lateef said. He seemed to relax.

"Then you can consider us your friends, too," Patrick said.

Lateef took the fish from Beth. He said, "I will allow it for now. But a time will come when all will sacrifice to our gods. They must be made happy."

Lateef clenched his teeth and hurried around the cousins. They followed along behind him.

Patrick whispered to Beth, "Why would anybody worship gods who are mad all the time?"

"I don't know," Beth said. "It makes me glad that I have a God who loves me."

They went back to the temple. Lateef made his sacrifice. Then they passed back through the crowd.

Lateef was treated like a king himself when they arrived at his home. Servants came from everywhere to ask if he needed anything. He raised his hand to quiet them. "Just tell me where my father is," he said.

"He is in the throne room," one of the servants said. "But he is talking with his advisers."

"Talking about what?" Lateef asked.

"The pharaoh is very busy protecting Egypt from its enemies," the servant said.

Lateef said, "Two men tried to force Tabitha out of her house. Is Tabitha's family now our enemy?"

The servant looked worried. "Perhaps you should ask your father. Of course, you must wait until he finishes his important meeting."

The servant bowed and left the cousins and Lateef alone in the huge, beautiful room. Patrick marveled at the colorful pictures on the walls. The air didn't smell like sweat and dead fish. It smelled like perfume.

Lateef waved a hand at them. "We'll wait on the roof. It's cooler there."

Lateef took them to a narrow stone staircase. They climbed up and came out on a flat roof.

Patrick expected it to be hot. But the walls surrounding them actually caught a cool breeze. They sat under a cloth canopy.

From here they could see much of the city. People scurried around. They all seemed upset and scared.

Lateef looked worried too.

After a few minutes, they heard a scuffle below them. Lateef stood up. He moved to the edge of the roof and looked down. Patrick and Beth joined him.

Near the palace entrance, a muscular man shouted at a teenage boy. Patrick couldn't understand the man's words.

The teenage boy dropped to his knees. He pleaded with the muscular man.

"What's going on?" Beth asked.

Lateef said, "I don't know. But I know that boy. It's Tabitha's older brother. He works—*worked* here as an errand boy."

Suddenly, the man pulled out a long, thin rope. He lashed the teenage boy's back with it.

"Aaahhh!" the boy screamed.

Lateef leaned forward. Beth looked worried that he might fall off the roof.

"What are you doing?" Lateef yelled. But the muscular man didn't hear him.

The boy raised his arm. The muscular man stopped the beating. The boy got up slowly. He could barely stand. The man raised the rope again.

"Stop!" Lateef shouted.

The muscular man looked up.

"Let him go!" Lateef demanded.

The man bowed and then walked away. The boy looked up at Lateef thankfully. Then the boy ran away on shaky legs.

"I must talk to my father, *now*! I will use the secret stairs," Lateef said.

Lateef and the cousins left the roof. They went down the stairs to a different hall. They reached a section of a wall with paintings of flowers.

Lateef pushed on one of the flowers. *Click.* A crack appeared in the wall. He pushed open the hidden door. It led to a secret staircase.

The three children went down the stairs.

They came to another wall. Lateef touched a stone, and a door opened. It led to a large room.

The room looked empty. Voices echoed

from somewhere.

Hieroglyphics had been painted on the walls and columns. A few brightly colored rugs covered the polished stone floors.

"Be silent," Lateef said softly. "This is the throne room."

The children crept around a pillar to see what was happening.

A thin man with a tall blue crown sat on a stone seat. The man held a golden scepter with a hook on the end. Patrick guessed the man was Lateef's father, the pharaoh.

The pharaoh was scolding a man. Patrick couldn't hear the words clearly. The pharaoh sounded angry—and maybe even a little afraid.

"I will have to speak," Lateef whispered.

He looked as if he might step forward.

Suddenly a man appeared in front of him. The man was carrying a tray of half-eaten food and dirty plates.

"Don't interrupt your father right now," the man said to Lateef.

"Hasheput!" Lateef said softly. "What are you doing here?"

"Serving your father, as I've always done," the man said. "Now leave quickly before you find yourself in trouble."

"I want to know what's happening," Lateef said.

"I'll tell you what I can," Hasheput said. "Follow me."

Hasheput led Lateef and the cousins through a back door to a courtyard. Past the courtyard was an area filled with workers. Some were washing clothes in basins.

Hasheput called out to a man and held up the tray. The man came and took it away.

"That's my friend Hasheput," Lateef said to Beth and Patrick. "He knows Tabitha's father."

Hasheput turned to the young prince. He looked troubled. "How may I serve you?" he asked.

"Why are there beatings?" asked Lateef. "Why is my father treating the Habiru like they're our enemies? Even now Tabitha!"

Hasheput looked around nervously. Then he seemed to be calm. "Your father doesn't trust any Habiru. He believes the Habiru are having too many children.

He's afraid they'll soon outnumber the Egyptians," Hasheput said.

"But it's good to have many friends," Lateef said.

"Friends, yes," Hasheput said. "But what if the Habiru realize their numbers and strength? What if they decide to attack? We couldn't defend ourselves."

"They have been friends to us for generations. They live among us," Lateef said. "What can my father do? Drive them all away? Destroy them?"

"No," Hasheput said. "His plan is to use them. Keep our power over them. Thousands have already been taken. They will be our slaves."

Lateef's eyes widened.

Beth gasped. "Slaves!"

The Slaves

Lateef's anger spilled out. "I cannot bear it! I won't allow Tabitha to become a slave," he said.

Beth thought Lateef was in a difficult position. How could he help his friend without disobeying his father?

"If you have no further need of me—" Hasheput said. He bowed and walked away.

"How can we help?" Beth asked Lateef.

"Find Tabitha or her father or her brother

Ammon," Lateef said.

"Ammon was the young man being beaten?" Beth asked.

"Yes. If you find them, they may come here. I'll hide them in the palace," Lateef said.

"Where will we find them?" Patrick asked. "At home?"

Lateef shook his head. "Their home is too dangerous. They may be among their own people."

"Where is that?" Beth asked.

"Go to the workers digging the canal," Lateef answered. "I will hope to speak with my father soon."

The three of them parted.

Beth and Patrick followed a well-worn path away from the palace. They asked a merchant in the marketplace where they could find the Habiru. He pointed toward a spot far away, next to the Nile.

"This won't be easy," Patrick said.

He was right. The hot sun blazed down on them. It felt as if someone had placed a hot iron on Beth's neck. The farther the cousins walked, the hotter they felt.

Patrick and Beth walked keeping watch. They searched in all directions for Tabitha or her brother.

Beth shook her feet. She had burning sand in her sandals.

"Look!" Patrick said to Beth. A crowd of people was hard at work. Most of them were dressed in simple tunics. They didn't have golden belts and necklaces like Beth and Patrick.

Many dug with shovels. Beth and Patrick

got closer. People were digging a long, deep hole.

"What are they doing?" Patrick asked.

"This must be the canal," Beth said. "It will come from the Nile. Boats come down the river. Then the boats can follow the canal and travel into the city. The canal will also allow water to flow into the desert."

"So this is why the Egyptians want slaves," Patrick said.

Beth felt sorry for everyone who worked hard shoveling dirt. Sweat poured down their sunburned faces.

A man near them doubled over and fell to his knees. Beth thought he must be suffering from the heat. She and Patrick ran toward him.

Before they reached him, an Egyptian

guard stepped forward. He held a long staff. He tapped it against the man's shoulder.

"Get up!" the guard shouted.

The man struggled to stand. The Egyptian quickly grabbed him and yanked him to his feet. The man's legs wobbled. He could barely stand.

"Dig!" the Egyptian shouted. The man bent over to pick up the shovel. Then he fell back to his knees. The Egyptian hit the man in the back with the staff.

"Hey!" Patrick yelled and moved forward. Beth grabbed his arm to hold him back. She was afraid of what the Egyptian would do.

The Egyptian guard scowled at Patrick. Then he turned back to the fallen man. "Get up!" the guard shouted.

The man was on all fours. Then a girl

hurried toward the man with a pot of water. It was Tabitha!

Tabitha put the pot down. She tilted the pot. Water trickled out. The man cupped his hands to catch the water. He slurped the liquid. Some of the water dripped down his chin.

"Be strong," Tabitha said to the man.

The Egyptian guard shoved Tabitha aside. "He's lazy. Away with you!" he said.

Tabitha backed away from the Egyptian. She looked sadly at the man on the ground. Beth and Patrick moved toward Tabitha.

Beth asked, "They've made you into a slave?"

"They caught me after you left my house," Tabitha said.

"Where is your family?" Beth asked.

Tabitha shook her head sadly. "They're digging," she said.

"Come with us," Patrick said. "Lateef said he would hide you in the palace."

Tabitha glanced around at the Egyptian guards. Some of them had whips.

"Meet me by the large water pots in those tents," Tabitha explained. She pointed to a set of open-air tents. Beth saw four enormous pots that looked like vases.

The cousins nodded. Tabitha took her small pot of water and raced away.

"What can we do?" Beth asked Patrick.

"I think I have a plan," Patrick said.

Beth and Patrick found Tabitha behind the tent. Patrick looked inside one of the large pots. "This one's empty," he said. "Can you fit in here?"

"What?" Tabitha asked.

"Get in the pot," Patrick said. "Beth and I will carry you to the palace."

"What?" Beth and Tabitha said at the same time.

Patrick picked up two poles lying nearby. He said, "We'll put these poles through the handles of the pot. Beth and I will carry the poles on our shoulders."

"It'll be hard," Tabitha said.

Patrick nodded. "Is there a better idea?"

There wasn't. Tabitha squeezed into the large pot.

Beth was surprised that Tabitha fit. Beth stood behind the pot, and Patrick stood in front of it. They both put the poles on their shoulders. They lifted the pot and carried it.

They passed by many slaves. They passed

by many Egyptian guards with whips. The Egyptians never looked at Patrick and Beth.

It was working!

Beth groaned. "Patrick, this is getting really heavy," she said.

"We'll slow down," he said.

Patrick was breathing heavily now. Sweat poured down his head, his neck, and his back.

Suddenly, Beth's foot hit a rock. She stumbled. The pot dropped. It cracked in half. Tabitha spilled out onto the dirt.

The noise caused heads to turn. An Egyptian guard saw the whole thing. He stomped over to them.

He said, "What's going on here?"

The Cell

Beth and Patrick stood silent.

Tabitha didn't say a word either. She sat on the sand. She looked scared.

The Egyptian looked first at Patrick and Beth. Then he scowled at the broken pot and the poles. He slowly shook his head.

"Back to work," he said to Tabitha. She looked helplessly at the cousins. Then she ran off.

The guard grabbed Beth and Patrick by

the shoulders. He said, "You two are coming with me."

"Where are you taking us?" Patrick asked.

The guard grunted and pushed the cousins toward a wooden cart. It had two oxen hitched to the front.

The Egyptian motioned for Patrick and Beth to climb into the back of the cart. He grabbed a rope from inside the cart. He tied the cousins' wrists together. The knots were tight. Then he looped the rope through the slats on the side of the cart.

"This will hold you," he said. He walked to the front of the cart and climbed on. He picked up a stick with a whip at the end.

Crack! The guard snapped the whip in the air. "Yah!" he said.

One of the oxen snorted. Then the

animals jerked the cart forward.

Patrick and Beth looked at each other. There was nothing to say.

They passed palms, rocks, statues, and ponds covered with blue lotus flowers. After a long time, they reached the front of a building. The guard stopped the cart.

Beth nodded toward the marketplace next to the building. "We're back again," she said.

The guard untied the rope from the cart. Then he used the rope to lead the cousins inside by their wrists.

The building was dark and smelled damp and sweaty. Patrick was glad to be out of the sun. The three of them walked down a long staircase. A door with metal bars was at the bottom.

It was a prison cell.

"No!" Beth cried. She pulled back.

The guard pushed her toward the door. "You were attempting to help a slave escape," he said.

He opened the cell door with a key. He roughly pushed the cousins inside.

Beth fell to her knees on wet straw.

Patrick stumbled and fell against a stone wall. Before he could turn around, he heard a *bang!* and then a *clank.*

"Tell Lateef we're here!" Patrick called out.

The guard walked away.

Patrick and Beth were locked in.

"So they're throwing children into prison now?" came a voice from the corner of the cell.

Beth gasped. Patrick whirled around.

An old man with a white beard came forward. His face was wrinkled. He looked as if he had been in the bathtub too long. His legs were as skinny as water pipes.

"My name is Malachi," the old man said. "Why are you here?"

Beth answered, "We tried to help a friend."

"A Habiru?" he asked.

Patrick nodded.

"Helping the Habiru is an easy way to get into trouble. That is why I'm in here," Malachi said.

"What did you do?" Patrick asked.

"I'm a teacher," Malachi said. "I taught the Habiru to read and to know their history."

"You were thrown into prison for teaching?" Patrick asked.

"The Egyptians didn't like my kind

of teaching," Malachi said. "It gave the Habiru hope. Where there is hope, there is strength."

"How do you give them hope?" Beth asked.

"By reminding them of their past," Malachi said. "And the way God has blessed them since the beginning."

Malachi gestured to the cell. "This very prison cell is part of Habiru history."

"I don't see a lot of hope here," Patrick said.

"How is it part of their history?" Beth asked.

"A Habiru man named Zaphenat-Pa'aneah was once imprisoned here," Malachi said.

"Zaf . . . " Beth said. "Who?"

Malachi shook his head. "You don't know of the great vizier?" he asked.

"What's a vi-ZEER?" Patrick asked.

Malachi looked startled. "What are they teaching children these days?" he asked. He shook his head. "Do you understand these pictures?" Malachi pointed to drawings on the wall.

"Those are hieroglyphics," Beth said. "Like the ones in here." She pulled the book out of her tunic. She opened the pages.

Malachi hurried to look at the book. "Where did you get that parchment?" Malachi asked. His fingers felt the pages. "The papyrus is so thin."

"Um . . . well . . . "

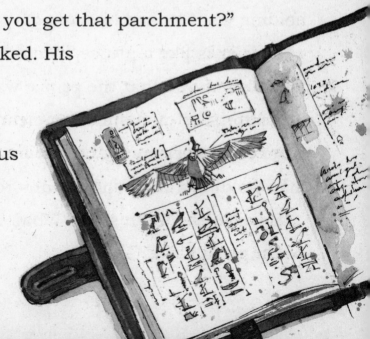

Beth said, "this is a special parchment."

The old man flipped through some of the pages. Then he stopped. "Here it is," he said, pointing at a drawing on a page.

Beth and Patrick looked at the drawing.

Beside the drawing was written the word *vizier*. The picture was an oval with three images inside it. The first image was a bird. Then there was a man standing. The last image was a man sitting down. He was holding what looked like a flag.

"A vizier is like a prince," Malachi said. "The bird shows that the prince was a protector. The man standing means that a vizier rules over men. The last image is of a man holding a flail. That means royalty."

"Excuse me," Beth said. "What is the man holding again?"

"A flail," Malachi said. "It's used for harvesting grains."

"What happened to the Habiru prince?" Patrick asked.

"He died long ago," Malachi said. "Our new pharaoh has taken the throne by force. He doesn't know about the great prince. He doesn't trust the Habiru. He's afraid they will rise up against him."

"Will they?" Patrick asked.

The old man shrugged. "I've never heard them speak of it," he said. "They're happy here."

"Someone needs to tell the pharaoh right away," Beth said.

"He has been told. But he won't listen," Malachi said. "Meanwhile, the Habiru are losing hope because they are slaves. They don't remember their past—or their prince."

Footsteps clopped down the stairs to the prison cell. Beth and Patrick looked up.

The lock rattled, and the door was yanked open. An Egyptian guard stepped in. Following him was Lateef.

"Lateef!" the cousins cried out. They moved toward him.

"This wasn't part of our plan," Lateef said with a frown. "The guard informed me you were here."

"Thank you," Beth said to the guard.

The guard nodded.

"We saw Tabitha," Patrick said to Lateef. "She's a slave."

Lateef eyed the guard. "Leave us," the pharaoh's son said with a wave of his arm. The guard obeyed.

"Where is she?" Lateef asked the cousins.

"She's working on the canal," Beth said. "She delivers water."

"That isn't so bad," Lateef said. He looked down sadly. "My father has forbidden me to help the Habiru—even Tabitha."

"Then what can we do?" Beth asked.

"I cannot help you," Lateef said. "I will set you free this time. But you can't help Tabitha or any of the Habiru. If you do, you'll pay the penalty. Perhaps prison or even death."

"We understand," Patrick said. "Thank you for getting us out this time."

Lateef lifted his head. He looked as if he might cry. He spun around and left the prison cell. The door remained open.

Beth moved toward the old man. "What

about you?" she asked.

"I'm not allowed to leave," Malachi said. "But please, go to the Habiru people. Remind them of their prince."

"But surely you heard Lateef," Patrick said.

Beth interrupted him. "We'll try," she said.

The cousins said good-bye to Malachi and left the cell.

Outside, Patrick said to Beth, "You said we would try to help the Habiru. Didn't you listen to Lateef's warning? If we get caught, we could get locked up again—or killed!"

Beth looked at him. "I still think we have to try."

"Try to do what?" Patrick asked.

"To give them hope," she said.

The Habiru

The cousins left the prison. They trudged through the marketplace toward the river. Beth was relieved that Patrick led the way.

They passed the same palms and statues and ponds. Only the lotus flowers had changed. They had closed and sunk into the water for the night.

The sun was setting. It was cooler now. Beth worried about what would happen once the sun went down. She knew the desert could be very cold at night.

The cousins finally arrived at the canal work zone. None of the slaves or guards were working.

Nearby, a group of tents had been set up. The tents glowed, lit up by fires inside.

Beth and Patrick went to the closest tent. They asked the people inside where Tabitha's family lived. The cousins were directed to another tent at the end of a long row.

The tent was large. When the cousins entered, they were faced with a crowd of a dozen people. Everyone turned to them.

Tabitha rushed over to Patrick and Beth.

"God be praised. You're safe!" Tabitha said. "My family has been praying for you."

Tabitha introduced Patrick and Beth

to her family—brothers, sisters, cousins, aunts, and uncles.

Patrick and Beth learned many names. They also heard about everyone's aches and pains. Some had been enslaved for weeks.

The Habiru's bodies were sore from the hard labor. Their skin was scorched. A few people were bent over sick. The tent smelled of sweat and blood.

A woman put a wet cloth over a man's injured knee.

"I won't survive another day," one older Habiru man said.

"This has been a horrible day," Tabitha said. "My brother Ammon was whipped by a guard."

"We know," Beth said.

Ammon lay on his side. He was very still.

Tabitha rolled up a cloth and gently placed it under his head.

Then Tabitha put a hand to her ear. "Do you hear that?" she asked.

Beth and Patrick listened. People all over the tent city were crying and groaning. The sounds pierced Beth's heart.

"Our God has forgotten us," a nearby woman named Miriam said.

"No, He hasn't," Beth said to her.

"Don't be foolish, child," Miriam said. "Our people are slaves. God has abandoned us."

"You're not abandoned," Beth said. "Don't you remember what happened before?"

"The *prince*?" Patrick added.

Everyone in the tent stopped talking or groaning and listened.

"We remember the prince," Tabitha said.

"He was my great-great-great-grandfather."

"Really?" Patrick asked.

Tabitha nodded. "That's why my family was able to live in a beautiful home. And why my father has—had—such a good job," she said.

Miriam shook her head. She said, "We remember the prince. But he was laid inside his tomb long ago. What good is he to us now?"

"His memory reminds you that God watched over you in the past," Beth said. "And He's watching over you now."

Miriam snorted and turned away.

"If only the great prince were here for us to see," Tabitha said.

"Where is his tomb?" Patrick asked. "Why don't you visit it? That will help you remember."

"The Egyptians won't let us near it," Tabitha's father said. "They know what remembering him will do for us."

"They've probably taken away the mummy and destroyed it," another man said. His name was Abner, and he had the injured knee. "They would do that just to show how much they hate us."

Miriam sighed. "The Egyptians treat the living with disrespect. Why wouldn't they do the same to the dead?"

"If only we could bring the mummy of the prince here," Tabitha said. "We could keep it safe. It would inspire our people."

"How would we do that?" Abner asked. "The tomb is in the necropolis."

"The what?" Patrick asked.

"Necropolis means 'city of the dead,'"
Abner said. "It's a huge graveyard where the
pharaohs and great leaders are buried."

Beth shivered at the thought.

Patrick asked, "Where is the necropolis
exactly?"

"The cliffs," Tabitha's father said. "To the
west of the tallest pyramid."

"But it's guarded," Miriam said. "The
Egyptians believe that whoever opens a
tomb will be cursed."

Beth glanced at Patrick. He looked as if
he had an idea.

"Aren't we already cursed by being slaves?"
Tabitha asked.

Tabitha's family nodded.

"How would a person get inside the tomb?"
Patrick asked.

"You must enter the vault and find the wall. There's a secret panel on the tomb's door," Abner said. "It's low, covered by sand. If you slide open the panel . . ."

"If you slide open the panel . . . then what?" Patrick asked.

"No one knows," Miriam said. "No one has ever gone inside."

Later that night the cousins lay on the ground to sleep. Beth whispered, "We can't do it."

"Yes we can," Patrick said. "You said you wanted to give these people hope."

"I meant by talking to them," Beth said. "Not by looking for mummies with Egyptian curses."

"I don't believe in curses," Patrick said.

"Okay, but are you really going to break into a tomb, steal a mummy, and carry it all the way back to the Habiru camp?" Beth asked.

"I've read that mummies aren't very heavy. They're just dried bones and some strips of cloth," Patrick said.

"But it's disgusting," Beth said.

"You heard Tabitha," Patrick said. "It'll inspire them."

Beth lay silently and thought about it. The Habiru needed to know that their prince's body was safe and honored.

Beth sighed deeply. She asked, "How are we going to do it?"

Patrick sat up and smiled at her. "I have no idea," he said.

The City of the Dead

Patrick and Beth hid behind a small hill. They lay on their stomachs and peeked over the hilltop. The morning sun was already baking them.

The vault was a stone's throw away. It was near a pyramid that was about twenty feet tall.

There was a problem, though. Two guards stood at the vault entrance. They looked stern and unhappy.

"How can we get inside with the guards watching?" Beth asked. "They'll throw us in prison for good this time."

Patrick looked thoughtful. "I don't know," he said.

"We need a diversion," Beth said.

"Like what?" Patrick asked.

"Beats me," she said with a shrug. "Something that will get them away from the door."

"How about that?" Patrick asked, pointing toward the pyramid.

A camel train came around the corner of the pyramid. It looked like the camel train they had seen at the marketplace. Five Egyptian traders were with the animals.

The guards turned to watch. The traders came within hearing distance. They called out to the guards. The guards looked around and then walked toward the traders.

"They must be offering the guards a good deal," Patrick said.

The vault entrance was now unguarded.

Patrick and Beth sneaked out from behind the hill. They crouched down and quietly headed for the vault entrance.

The door to the tomb was behind three pillars. The pillars held up an arched roof. The cousins hid behind the pillars and glanced at the guards. They were still busy bargaining with the traders.

Patrick tugged at Beth's sleeve, and they went through the open doorway.

Inside, an oil lamp was the only light. It rested in a hole in the wall. The lamp looked like a bowl filled with water. Patrick lifted it out of the hole.

The passageway in front of them was dark. The lamplight showed spiderwebs crisscrossing the walls.

Beth gulped. "Hold the lamp up," she said. "I don't want to be surprised by anything gross."

Patrick lifted the lamp. Beth could see his face. His expression seemed uneasy.

The hallway had steps leading down to pitch-black darkness.

The cousins slowed.

"Are you sure about this?" Beth asked.

They moved down the stairs.

Beth carefully split the spiderwebs with her hand. She didn't want anything to creep up on her suddenly. But the lamp was dim. She could see only a few feet ahead.

Suddenly, Beth heard a chilling moan. She gasped.

"Don't worry," Patrick said. "It's the wind. Like air blowing across the top of a glass bottle."

Beth nodded. But she still didn't like it.

Patrick and Beth ducked under a beam in the passageway.

"May I have the lamp?" Beth asked.

Patrick handed it to her. She lifted it to light up the hieroglyphics covering the walls and ceiling.

"Wow," she said.

"Let's keep moving," Patrick said.

Beth held the lamp with both hands.

Slowly . . . slowly . . . they walked.

The stairs continued at a gentle slope deep underground.

Finally, Beth saw a wide square column
in front of her. Patrick saw it too and walked
ahead of her.

They heard voices from outside.

"The guards!" Patrick whispered.

The cousins rushed into the darkness.

The Prince's Tomb

Beth heard Patrick stumble. Her throat tightened. It was all she could do not to scream too. She lowered the oil lamp. The light spread across the floor.

"Patrick?" she whispered. "Are you okay?"

"Help!" he gasped. Patrick was dangling by one arm from the edge of a hole.

Beth put down the lamp and grabbed his wrist. She pulled hard.

Patrick didn't budge. He was too heavy.

"I just need to get an elbow on the ledge. Then I can pull myself up," Patrick said.

She reached down again. Beth pulled with all her might. "Hnnggg!" she grunted. It felt as if her arms were going to tear off.

Patrick was now up far enough. He hooked an elbow onto the top of the ledge. Then the other elbow. He scrambled to pull his body up.

Beth collapsed backward. But at least Patrick was safe.

Beth and Patrick breathed hard. Patrick gave Beth a quick "thank you" smile.

Beth smiled back, but her heart was still pounding from the fright. *Maybe this wasn't such a good idea,* she thought.

Beth shifted position. Then she lowered the lamp toward the hole. She gasped.

The hole was very deep. If
Patrick had fallen in, he would have
disappeared into the darkness.

Patrick knelt next to her and whistled
softly. He picked up a stone and dropped
it. It fell for a few seconds before making a
distant *splash*.

"It's a well," Beth said. Her eye fell on a
rope with a bucket tied to it.

"I guess I should walk slower from now on," Patrick said.

The cousins stood up. They brushed themselves off and looked around.

Just beyond the hole was a room with four giant pillars. Every wall had hieroglyphics on it. The outline of a door was cut into a wall.

Patrick said, "Maybe this is the prince's tomb."

Beth thumbed through her hieroglyphics book. "I don't see any of the drawings for the vizier," Beth said. "It's probably someone else's tomb."

"Let's go that way," Patrick said. He pointed to a distant hallway.

They headed down a long passageway that twisted and turned. They reached an intersection.

"Which way?" Patrick said. "Left or right?"

"How am I supposed to know?" Beth asked. "Pick one."

Patrick led the way to the left. They rounded a corner and came to a solid wall. "It doesn't go any farther," Patrick said.

"Why would a passageway lead to nothing but a wall?" Beth asked.

"It's like a maze," Patrick said.

"Maybe it *is* a maze," Beth suggested.

"To confuse grave robbers," Patrick said.

The cousins doubled back and searched the long hallways. Beth checked for clues. But none of the walls had the right pictures or symbols.

Patrick and Beth descended deeper and deeper into the vault.

"Stop," Beth said suddenly. She held up the lamp. "There!"

Patrick looked up. There was an oval with a bird and a kneeling man in it. But there was no man in the middle, like the other picture. Instead, there was a funny-looking tree.

"This is it," Beth said.

"It's close, but it's not the same," Patrick said. "We'll have to keep looking."

"Wait," Beth said. "Look at the clothes on the people on the wall. They aren't Egyptian white tunics. They look like the Habiru's clothes."

"If this is it, then there must be a panel around here," Patrick said. "The Habiru man said it was low."

Patrick got down on his hands and knees.

Patrick scooped away the sand. His fingers searched the wall for the edge of the panel.

"I found it!" he said. He slid open the panel.

Beth lowered the lamp so Patrick could get a better look. "What's inside?" she asked.

"A rope," Patrick said.

"Don't pull it," Beth said. "It could be a trap. Sand could come pouring out. Or a big stone block could fall on us."

"What are we supposed to do?" Patrick asked. "Wait here for the prince to open the door for us? I don't think so."

He pulled the rope.

Part of the wall in front of them opened a few inches. It was a door. Patrick pushed on it with his shoulder.

"Help me," he said. The cousins pushed on

the door together. It opened slowly.

They entered a chamber. Patrick took the lamp from Beth and held it up high. The chamber was full of furniture and vases, statues and urns.

Beth's mouth fell open at all the riches.

"There!" Patrick said.

A large wooden box was at the back of the room. It was covered with beautiful colors.

"Wow!" Patrick said. "This is his coffin!"

Beth looked it over carefully. "It's not like the coffin of King Tut that I've seen in books," she said.

Patrick felt around the edges of the coffin. "There has to be a way to open it," he said.

Beth continued studying the colorful coffin. Then she took out her book and checked the hieroglyphics.

"Can you help me with this, Beth?" Patrick asked. "The lid is stuck."

She didn't hear him. She was deep in thought. Finally she said, "Look at the coat on the coffin."

Patrick stopped to look. "What about it?" he asked.

"Remember the tree symbol? I think it's supposed to be wheat," Beth said.

"What do you mean?" Patrick asked.

"Do you remember the story from Sunday school? About the coat of many colors?" Beth asked.

Patrick gazed at the coffin. "Sure," he said. "That's the story about Joseph."

Beth asked, "Do you remember what happened to Joseph?"

"Yes," Patrick said. "The Old Testament

says he was thrown into a pit by his brothers. They sold him into slavery. Then he was thrown into jail in Egypt . . ." Patrick paused as if he were thinking about something important.

"Then he became the second-in-command to Pharaoh," Beth said. "He saved the country from famine. He had the Egyptians store grain for seven years."

"The prince who saved Egypt," Patrick said. He stepped closer to the coffin and traced the symbols with his finger. "Why didn't we figure it out before? He was the vizier of wheat."

Beth said, "This is the tomb of Joseph!"

The Prince's Bones

"Yes," Patrick said. "It all makes sense. The Habiru are the *Hebrews*. God's chosen people in the Old Testament."

Beth's eyes lit up. "Joseph was a Hebrew. That's why he gave special treatment to his people. That's why they've been treated well for generations," she said.

"And that's why Tabitha lived in that nice house," Patrick said. "Because she was Joseph's relative."

Beth suddenly remembered the story from the Bible. "This is the time leading up to Moses," she said.

"The Hebrews are just starting hundreds of years of slavery," Patrick said. "They won't be freed until Moses leads them to the Promised Land."

Patrick paused and then said, "Moses . . . Wait a minute!"

Patrick reached into his tunic. He pulled out his Bible. He had forgotten to read the page with the bookmark.

"Exodus 13:19," he read. "Moses took the bones of Joseph with him because Joseph had made the Israelites swear an oath."

Patrick closed the Bible. "When Moses left Egypt, the Hebrews took the bones of Joseph with them," Patrick said.

Beth smiled. "So the Hebrews don't have to worry about Joseph's mummy," she said. "It'll be safe until Moses comes to get it."

"That's right," Patrick said. "God's going to take care of everything."

Beth said, "That's what we need to tell the Hebrews. Even though things are hard now, God is looking out for His people."

Patrick smiled and patted the coffin.

"Does that mean we don't have to take Joseph's mummy?" Beth asked.

"We can't," Patrick said. "It has to stay here for Moses. That's a long time ahead."

They both breathed a sigh of relief.

Beth led the way out of the tomb chamber.

Suddenly, a light came toward them.

"Stop!" said a man's voice. "What are you doing here?"

The Maze

"What should we do?" Beth asked Patrick.

Patrick seemed frozen where he was.

The big Egyptian came closer. The torch in his hand lit up his lined face.

Suddenly Patrick called out, "This way!" Beth obeyed.

Patrick ducked down a passageway.

"Where are you going?" Beth asked, still running.

"I'm good at mazes," Patrick said. "I can

get us out of here."

Beth hoped he was right.

Patrick darted around corners. Beth followed. They stopped and listened. The passageway was perfectly quiet.

Patrick looked at the lamp in Beth's hand.

"He'll see the light," Patrick said. "You have to put it out."

"Are you crazy?" Beth asked. "You want to run around this place in the dark?"

"I remember the maze, Beth," Patrick said. "Trust me."

Beth looked at the lamp. She said a small prayer asking God to help Patrick's memory. Then she dropped the lamp on the ground. The flame went out.

Beth couldn't see Patrick. She couldn't even see her hand in front of her face.

"Hold on to my tunic," Patrick said. "This way."

Beth could hear Patrick feeling the walls with his hands. He moved slowly.

They could hear the guard moving around in another passageway. He shouted, "Surrender! I will find you!"

Beth could tell that he was getting closer.

The cousins walked more quickly, but they were still slow. They came to a corner and turned.

"Beth, do you hear that?" Patrick asked.

Beth listened carefully. It was a low moaning.

"It's the same sound we heard near the entrance," Patrick said.

"The stairs must be ahead. Watch out for the well."

"I have an idea," Beth said. She bent down on her hands and knees. She crawled until she felt the well opening. She felt around till she found the bucket and rope. The rope was fastened to a metal ring in the floor.

She picked up the bucket and lowered it into the water. Then she pulled the rope back up. She had a bucket full of water. It smelled of old earth.

She untied the rope from the bucket. "Stay here," Beth said to Patrick.

Beth moved away from him. She stood at the edge of the hallway and waited.

She peeked around the corner. She saw the light from the guard's torch coming closer . . . closer.

When the guard turned, she threw the water at him.

Splash!

The torch flame went out. The room went pitch-black. Beth heard the guard curse.

She hurried back over to Patrick. "Sit over there," she whispered. She huddled next to him.

The guard stumbled around in the darkness. "Where are you?" he called out.

The cousins sat quietly.

The guard came closer. His footsteps echoed through the passageway.

"I'm going to have your heads," the guard said. His voice echoed in front and behind the cousins.

Beth and Patrick barely breathed. The footsteps came closer.

Beth coughed a little on purpose.

The guard stopped in his tracks.

Beth heard him turn and then head straight toward them.

"Now I have you," the guard said. "Aaahhh!"

Sploosh! The guard fell into the well.

Beth shouted, "Let's go!"

"Wait," Patrick said. "We can't leave him."

Patrick tied the rope tightly to the bucket again. "He can use this to climb out. The rope is tied to the ring in the floor."

Patrick threw the bucket into the well. A second later, they heard it hit something.

"Ouch," the guard shouted.

"Come on, Beth," Patrick said. "This way."

Beth put her hands on Patrick's shoulder. The cousins hurried in the dark. They reached the stairs and made their way up.

Soon Beth could see a light in the distance. They reached the entrance.

The cousins paused to catch their breath. The doorway was only a few feet away.

Suddenly the second guard stepped in front of them. "Stop," the guard said.

Patrick pointed inside the vault. "Quick!" he said. "Your friend fell down a well. He's in trouble!"

The guard paused. He seemed to be deciding if Patrick's story was true.

Just then the guard in the well shouted.

The other guard made up his mind. He hurried into the passageway.

Patrick and Beth stepped outside the vault into daylight. They headed toward the Hebrew camp.

The Tent

"We went to Joseph's tomb," Patrick told Tabitha. "His bones are safe. And they're going to stay that way."

"What?" Tabitha asked.

Tabitha's family gathered around the cousins inside the tent. "How do you know?" a Hebrew man asked.

Patrick reached into his tunic and pulled out his Bible. "Look, I know it's hard to understand, but this book is called a Bible.

It's the Word of God. It tells the story of your prince Joseph. And it tells how one day another great prince will rescue you from slavery. God will lead you out of Egypt."

Some of Tabitha's family looked surprised. Others looked like they didn't believe Patrick.

Beth said, "Not today or tomorrow. But it will happen. You'll have to trust God. Just like Joseph did."

Patrick held up the Bible again. He said, "The prince was sold into slavery and sent to jail. But God still remembered him. Never give up hope."

"It would be easier if we had the prince's mummy here," Tabitha said.

"Your hope can't be in a dead man's dried-up body," Patrick said. "It has to be in God, who is *alive.*"

"That's what your great prince believed," Beth added.

Tabitha smiled. "You're right," she said. "God has always been faithful to us."

The old woman Miriam nodded. She said, "And we should remain faithful to Him."

Beth and Patrick smiled at Tabitha and her family.

A man in the back raised an instrument. It was orange and looked like a very skinny guitar. He strummed it a few times.

Then the Hebrew people began to sing a worship song to God: "Blessed are the people who trust in the Lord. O God, hear our prayers for safety and peace."

Beth and Patrick looked at each other. "I think our adventure is over," Patrick said.

As Tabitha's family sang to God, Patrick

and Beth quietly left the tent. Tabitha followed them out.

"Are you leaving us?" Tabitha asked.

Nearby, a whirring noise caught Beth's attention. It was the Imagination Station. Patrick saw it. Tabitha didn't seem to notice.

"It's time for us to go," Patrick said.

Tabitha hugged them both. Tears filled her eyes. "Thank you for reminding us of the truth," she said.

Patrick blushed. Beth beamed.

A voice called from inside the tent. "Tabitha, Ammon is awake!"

Tabitha's face lit up. "I must go," she said.

Beth and Patrick climbed into the Imagination Station.

They saw Tabitha waving good-bye.

Then Beth pushed the red button.

Whit's End

"Well?" Whit asked as Patrick and Beth climbed out of the Imagination Station.

Patrick said. "I was wrong to say that the slavery of the Hebrews is still like school."

"What about being teased for your faith?" Whit asked.

Patrick shook his head. "It's not as bad as the Hebrews had it."

"There was a more important lesson I

hope you learned," Whit said.

The cousins looked at each other.

Beth brightened with an idea. "I thought a lot about my faith in God," she said.

Patrick nodded. "We met the Hebrews when everything was about to go all wrong," he said. "They were about to spend a long time in slavery. But God still wanted them to keep their hope in Him."

"We tried to help Tabitha and her family understand that," Beth said.

"You did," Whit said. "Do you think *you* understand it better now?"

Patrick and Beth thought about it for a moment.

Patrick then said, "It's easy for people

to put their hope in the wrong thing when things go bad."

"Putting our hope in the right thing when times are bad is what counts, Beth said."

Whit smiled. "That's something to think about when it comes to school and being teased."

Beth said, "God wants me to have hope in Him, not in what happens to me."

"That's right," Whit said.

Patrick chuckled. "I wish school could teach us the way you do with these adventures."

"But these adventures can be hard work," Whit said. "You two have had some tough experiences."

"Yeah, but that's different," Beth said.

"Is it?" Whit asked. "Isn't learning math or science or English an adventure too?"

Beth grinned. "Only if we could do it at some other time in history," she said.

Whit laughed.

"Are there other adventures we can take to help us with school?" Patrick asked.

"I think we can come up with a few more," Whit said.

"Tomorrow?" Beth asked.

"Sure. Come back tomorrow," Whit said.

Questions about Egypt

Q: Why didn't this story talk more about the Great Pyramids and the Sphinx?

A: *Because those structures were built a thousand years before Joseph was born. Also, the Hebrews lived in a different area.*

Q: Why did the ancient Egyptians make mummies?

A: *To preserve bodies for the afterlife journey. Even poor people dried the bodies of their relatives in the sun.*

For more information about Egypt and the Hebrews, visit *TheImaginationStation.com*.

Secret Word Puzzle

Use the clues to fill in the puzzle on the next page. The letters in the shaded boxes will spell out a secret word.

Write those letters in the boxes below the puzzle grid. The answer is the secret word and the name of Joseph's birthplace.

1 The box where Joseph's bones were stored. (page 91)

2 The Egyptian goddess of the Nile River. (page 33)

3 Mr. Whittaker's first name. (page 1)

4 The title for an Egyptian king. (page 29)

5 A giant tomb in Egypt. These buildings are pointed at the top. (page 78)

6 Name of the famous Egyptian river. (page 30)

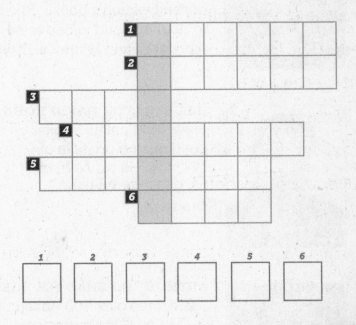

Go to **TheImaginationStation.com**
Find the cover of this book.
Click on "Secret Word."
Type in the correct answer,
and you'll receive a prize.

117

AUTHOR MARIANNE HERING
is the former editor of *Focus on the Family Clubhouse*® magazine. She has written more than a dozen children's books. She likes to read out loud in bed to her fluffy gray-and-white cat, Koshka.

ILLUSTRATOR DAVID HOHN
draws and paints books, posters, and projects of all kinds. He works from his studio in Portland, Oregon.

AUTHOR MARSHAL YOUNGER
has written over 100 Adventures in Odyssey® radio dramas and the children's book series Kidsboro. He lives in Tennessee with his wife and four children. He has been a Cleveland Indians fan for 34 long years.

NEW!

ADVENTURES IN ODYSSEY
8
FOCUS ON THE FAMILY PRESENTS
THE IMAGINATION STATION

Mystery of Starlight Island

MARIANNE HERING • WAYNE BATSON

The Imagination Station brings Patrick and Beth to the South Pacific in 1841. The cousins join the clever Scottish pirate hunter, Captain Connor Glenn and the crew of the flagship Saint Andrew's Lance.

The search for pirates leads Patrick and Beth to the emerald-green islands of Fiji where they attempt to rescue missionary William Cross. But when pirates attack the island, Patrick and Cross are kidnapped, Beth and Captain Glenn must race against time to save their two captive friends. The only hopes they have of rescue rest in their trust in God and a broken telescope, that just might reveal more than meets the eye.

FOCUS ON THE FAMILY®

No matter who you are, what you're going through, or what challenges your family may be facing, we're here to help. With practical resources —like our toll-free Family Help Line, counseling, and Web sites— we're committed to providing trustworthy, biblical guidance, and support.

Focus on the Family Clubhouse Jr.

Creative stories, fascinating articles, puzzles, craft ideas, and more are packed into each issue of *Focus on the Family Clubhouse Jr.*® magazine. You'll love the way this bright and colorful magazine reinforces biblical values and helps boys and girls (ages 3–7) explore their world. **Subscribe now at Clubhousejr.com.**

Focus on the Family Clubhouse

Through an appealing combination of encouraging content and entertaining activities, *Focus on the Family Clubhouse*® magazine (ages 8–12) will help your children—or kids you care about—develop a strong Christian foundation. **Subscribe now at Clubhousemagazine.com.**

Go to FocusOnTheFamily.com or call us at 800-A-FAMILY (232-6459)